Highlights **Puzzle Readers**

LEVEL
LET'S READ
TOGETHER
1

Nick and Nack
Fly a Kite

By Brandon Budzi
Art by Adam Record

HIGHLIGHTS PRESS

Honesdale, Pennsylvania

Stories + Puzzles = Reading Success!

Dear Parents,

Highlights Puzzle Readers are an innovative approach to learning to read that combines puzzles and stories to build motivated, confident readers.

Developed in collaboration with reading experts, the stories and puzzles are seamlessly integrated so that readers are encouraged to read the story, solve the puzzles, and then read the story again. This helps increase vocabulary and reading fluency and creates a satisfying reading experience for any kind of learner. In addition, solving Hidden Pictures puzzles fosters important reading and learning skills such as:

- shape and letter recognition

- letter–sound relationships

- visual discrimination

- logic

- flexible thinking

- sequencing

With high-interest stories, humorous characters, and trademark puzzles, Highlights Puzzle Readers offer a winning combination for inspiring young learners to love reading.

This is Nick.

This is Nack.

Nick loves to **make** things.
Nack loves to **find** things.
They make a good **team**.

You can help them
by solving the
Hidden Pictures
puzzles.

"I found the tape!" says Nack.

"We can use the tape
to put the kite together," says Nick.

"Can we also use glue?" asks Nack.

"Yes!" says Nick.

Help Nick and Nack.
Find 5 bottles of glue hidden in the picture.

Happy reading!

It is a windy day.

Nick and Nack watch

the trees blow in the wind.

"Look," says Nack.

"The wind blew sticks off the trees!"

"The yard is a mess!" says Nick.

"We can clean up the sticks,"

says Nack.

Nick and Nack go outside
to pick up the sticks.

"Look," says Nack.

"This stick is short."

"Look," says Nick.

"This stick is long."

"What can we do with

the sticks?" asks Nack.

"We can make a kite," says Nick.

"Then we can fly the kite."

"How can we make a kite?"

asks Nack.

"First, we need paper," says Nick.

"I can help find paper," says Nack.

Nick finds thick paper.

Nack finds thin paper.

"We can use the thin paper," says Nick.

"Thin paper will help the kite fly."

"Can we color on the paper?"
asks Nack.

"Yes!" says Nick.

Help Nick and Nack.
Find 5 crayons hidden in the picture.

"Now we need tape," says Nick.

"I can help find tape," says Nack.

They look in front of the books.

They look behind the books.

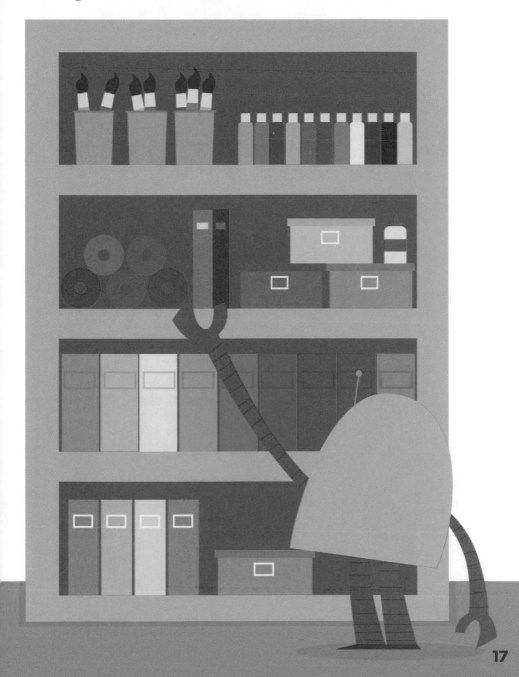

"I found the tape!" says Nack.

"We can use the tape
to put the kite together," says Nick.

"Can we also use glue?" asks Nack.

"Yes!" says Nick.

Help Nick and Nack.
Find 5 bottles of glue hidden in the picture.

"Now we need string," says Nick.

"I can help find string," says Nack.

Nack finds a sock.

He finds a spoon.

He finds a straw.

He cannot find string.

"Here is the string!" says Nack.

"We can add bows to the string," says Nick.

"That will look nice!" says Nack.

Help Nick and Nack.
Find 5 bows hidden in the picture.

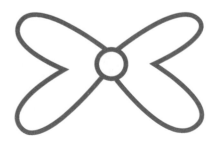

"Now let's make the kite!" says Nick.

They color the paper.

They glue the paper to the sticks.

They tie string to the kite.

"The kite is done,"

says Nack.

"Time to fly the kite!" says Nick.

"Oh, no!" says Nick.

"Now it is raining."

"Where did the sun go?"
says Nack.

Help Nick and Nack.
Find 5 suns hidden in the picture.

29

Fly Your Own KITE!

WHAT YOU NEED:

- **Tissue paper**
  You can also use newspaper or a plastic bag!
- **Sticks**
- **Tape or glue**
- **Markers**
- **String**
- **Ribbon**
- **Scissors**

1 MAKE A DIAMOND

- Fold thin paper in half.
- Use a marker to draw two lines, as shown.
- Cut on the lines, then unfold.

Make sure not to cut the fold!

2 FOLD THE EDGES

- Fold down about an inch on each side of the diamond.
- Tape down the corners.

You can decorate the kite with markers and stickers, or you can leave it plain.

3 MAKE A FRAME

- Make a T shape with the sticks.
- Cut the ends of the sticks to the size of the kite.
- Tape or glue the end of each stick to the four points.

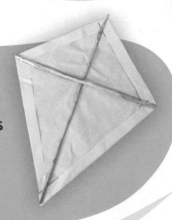

4 ADD STRING

- Cut a long piece of string.
- Tie one end to where the two sticks cross.
- Tie the other end to a small stick.
- Roll the extra string onto the stick.

5 ADD A TAIL

- Cut a piece of string and tie it to the bottom of the kite.
- Cut three pieces of ribbon.
- Tie each ribbon into a bow on the string tail.

Nick and Nack's TIPS

- Gather your supplies before you start crafting.
- Ask an adult or robot for help with anything sharp or hot.
- Clean up your workspace when your craft is done.

31

For information about permission to reprint
selections from this book, please contact
permissions@highlights.com.

Published by Highlights Press
815 Church Street
Honesdale, Pennsylvania 18431
ISBN (paperback): 978-1-64472-112-4
ISBN (hardcover): 978-1-64472-111-7
ISBN (ebook): 978-1-64472-225-1

Library of Congress Control Number: 2019941078
Manufactured in Melrose Park, IL, USA
Mfg. 09/2020

First edition
Visit our website at Highlights.com.
10 9 8 7 6 5 4 3 2 1 (pb)   10 9 8 7 6 5 4 3 2 (hc)

Craft by Elizabeth Wyrsch-Ba
Photos by Jim Filipski, Guy Cali Associates, Inc.

This book has been officially leveled by using the
F&P Text Level Gradient™ Leveling System.

LEXILE®, LEXILE FRAMEWORK®, LEXILE
ANALYZER®, the LEXILE® logo and POWERV® are
trademarks of MetaMetrics, Inc., and are registered
in the United States and abroad. The trademarks
and names of other companies and products
mentioned herein are the property of their
respective owners. Copyright © 2019
MetaMetrics, Inc. All rights reserved.

For assistance in the preparation of this book, the
editors would like to thank Vanessa Maldonado,
MSEd, MS Literacy Ed. K–12, Reading/LA Consultant
Cert., K–5 Literacy Instructional Coach; and Gina
Shaw.